A Tutu for Two

Nina sees a store.
TUTU SALE!
Hey!
What?
TUTU SALE!
Hey, Tina! Are you thinking what I am thinking?
I think so, Nina!

May I help you?
I hope so!
Me, too!
SALES
I am Nina!
And I am Tina!
We are ballerinas . . .
. . . and we need tutus!
You are at the right place.

Here is a very nice tutu.
Too long.
Yes, too long.
This tutu is nice, too.
Too short.
Yes, too short.

How about one of these?
Hmm . . .
Too plain.
Dressing Rooms
Too fancy.

Later that day:
Is that all you have?
Well, I do have one more.
This is the last one.
It is just right! I love it!
Me, too!

We will take two!
But I only have one.
Only one?
Do not hog the tutu!
Mine!
RIP!
Oops.

Hey, Tina! Are you thinking what I am thinking?
I think so, Nina!
TUTU STORE
COFFEE SHOP
Two tutus are better than one!
BANK

Star Search

I just love my new tutu!
CANDY STORE
Me, too!
DANCE TRYOUTS THIS WAY

Tina and Nina see a sign.
DANCE TRYOUTS THIS WAY
Hey!
BUMP!
Excuse me!
What?

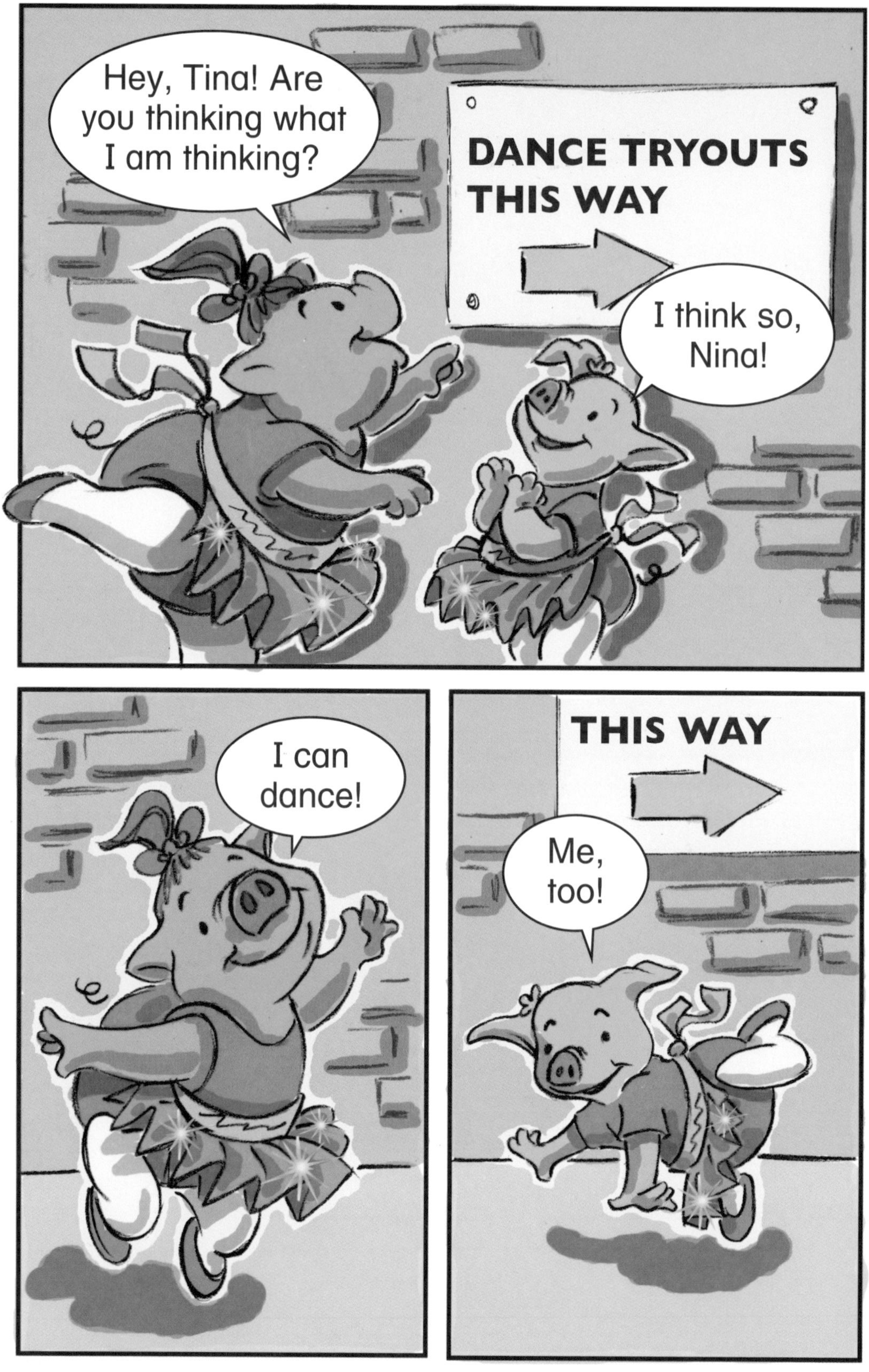
Hey, Tina! Are you thinking what I am thinking?
DANCE TRYOUTS THIS WAY
I think so, Nina!
I can dance!
THIS WAY
Me, too!

I want to be a star!
Me, too!
DANCE TRYOUTS THIS WAY
Here we go!
STAGE DOOR

Who is next?
Me!
Me, too!
WHACK!
Okay. Let me see what you can do.

Can you do this?
I can do that!
Me, too!
Look at me!
No, look at me!
BUMP!
CRASH!
Ugh!

How about this?
Oh, I can do that!
Oh, me, too!
Look at me!
No! Look at me!
SLAM!
THUD!
Can you make us stars?

Make you stars? When pigs fly!
But . . . we are the Tutu Twins!
Next!

AGE
OR
Well! I never!
Really! Me neither!
SLAM!

Some people do not know talent!
Too true!
BAM!
BEAR BOOKS
Hey! Watch it!

Stars Are Born

We can put on our own show!
BIG BIG SHOW TODAY
STARRING
Hmm.
STARRING
Hmm.

BIG
STARRIN
Nina
I think I should be the star.
BIG
ARRING
No. I think *I* should be the star.
We will see who will be the star.
BIG BIG SHOW TODAY
STARRING
Nina

Only a star could do this!
BOINK!
That hurt!
Only a star could do this!
BUMP!
Watch it!
And what about this?

Why do you always have to be so pig headed?
At last, it is show time.
Ta-da!
Gulp!

Nina and Tina run away!

Tina,
I am scared!
Me
too!

Are you
thinking what
I am thinking,
Tina?
I think so,
Nina.

We can be stars *together*!
After you, Tina.
No, after you, Nina!

The end . . .
CLAP! CLAP!
They really like us!
HOORAY!
. . . or just the beginning?
BRAVO
Two tutus *are* better than one!
CLAP!